It came through the wall!

It came through the wall!

Tim Healey
illustrated by Tony Ross

This edition published in the United States of American in 1996
by MONDO Publishing
First published in Great Britain in 1993 by Hutchinson Children's Books,
an imprint of Random House UK Limited

Text copyright © 1993 by Tim Healey
Illustrations copyright © 1993 by Tony Ross

For information contact:
MONDO Publishing
980 Avenue of the Americas
New York, New York 10018
Visit our web site at http:// www.mondopub.com

Printed in the United States of America
First Mondo Printing, January 2000
02 03 04 05   9 8 7 6

Library of Congress Cataloging-in-Publication data
Healey, Tim.
     It came through the wall / Tim Healey ; illustrated by Tony Ross.
        p. cm.
     Summary: A monster breaks through the wall and into the bedroom of
an imaginative child who finds a way to return the visit with a trip to
monsterland.
     ISBN 1-57255-213-1 (pb : alk. paper)
     [1. Monsters— Fiction. 2. Stories in rhyme.] I. Ross, Tony, ill. II. Title.
PZ7.H3445It   1996
[E]—dc20   96-15048
                                                               CIP
                                                               AC

Contents

PART 1

It came through the wall!
It came through the wall!
Oh horrible, horrible,
Hairy and all!

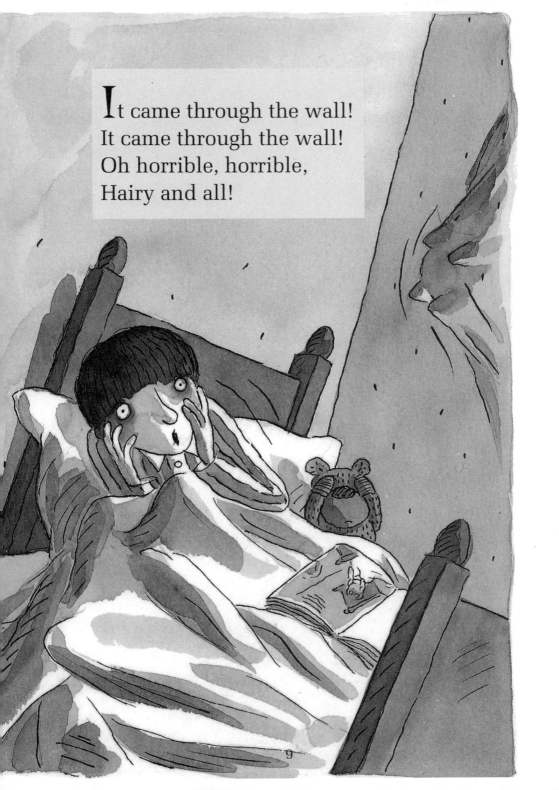

9

One finger came first,
But that wasn't the worst.
'Cause along came its friends
With claws on the ends!

Then came the whole hand,
The wrist, elbow, and —
Bolder and bolder —
The huge, hairy shoulder!

I lay in my bed,
In my panic and dread,
And I pulled all the bedclothes
Up over my head.

And I wanted to scream,
I wanted to shout,
But somehow the words
Just wouldn't come out.

All I managed to squeak
Was one stifled *Eek!*
And then, like a fool,
I took one more peek.

And it came through the wall!
It came through the wall!
Horrible, horrible,
Hairy and all!

Oh horrible, horrible,
Hairy and squinting,
With one eye shut tight
And the other one glinting.

Crouching down low,
It came in with a scuffle,
With a lisp and a slobbering
Sort of kerfuffle.

Then the Thing sort of wheezed
And rose up straight and tall,
The Whole Hideous Thing
Had come right through the wall!

Horrible, horrible,
Hairy as doom!
Hairy and hideous,
Inside my room!

And I wanted to die,
I just wanted to die,
To float off to the clouds
Way up in the sky.

But the Horrible Thing
Was not having that,
On the edge of my bed
The Thing horribly sat!

19

And then in a voice
Between slobber and croak,
The Thing cleared its throat
And it horribly spoke.

"I come from a land
That might give you a fright,
A place of great darkness,
Of shadowy night,

"Where swampish, mysterial
Mists wreathe the air,
And everyone goes around
Covered with hair.

"But I saw a dim light
And I felt the strange call
To seek out a bedroom
And walk through its wall.

"And now I have done it,
And now here I am.
You have seen that I'm neither
A fraud nor a sham,

But horrible, horrible,
Hairy and all!
And now I propose to go
Back through your wall."

And that's just what it did.
And before it went off
It delivered a sort of
Kerfuffly cough.

And then, almost shyly,
It said with a beam,
"Do remember, I'm not
Quite so bad as I seem."

Then it went through the wall.
It went with a shuffle,
A lisping and slobbering
Sort of kerfuffle.

And I tell you this,
Though it might seem insane...

PART 2

Where is the monster
Who gave me a fright?
That's what I asked myself
Night after night.

Where is the Thing
With the huge, hairy head?
Where is the monster
That sat on my bed?

I found myself feeling
Quite bored and alone,
Pacing the floor of
My monster-free zone.

Night after night
I pined and I moped
For a monster that never
Turned up, as I hoped.

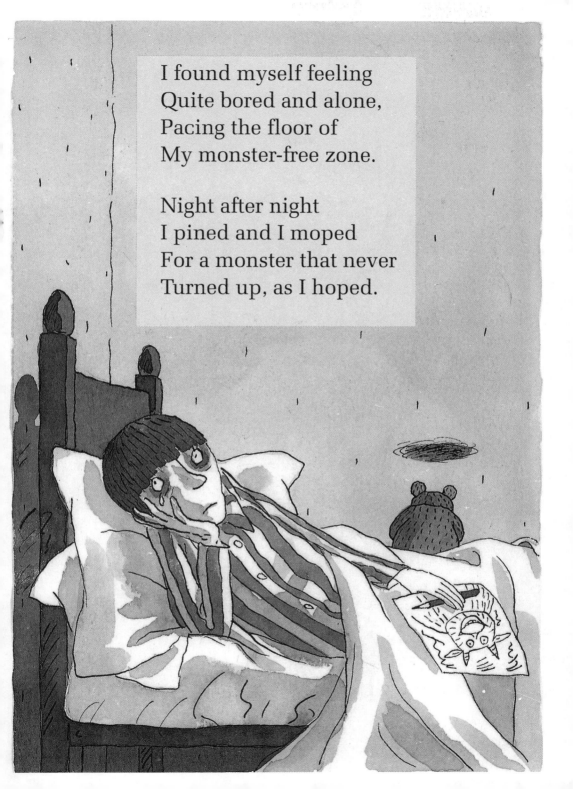

'Til one night in my bedroom
I gave a wild call,
Took one step backward,
And jumped through the wall!

I jumped through the wall!
I jumped through the wall!
With toothbrush, pajamas,
And slippers, and all!

I jumped through the wall!
I sailed through the air
To the land of the monsters
All covered with hair!

And dark was the sky
And soft was the ground
Where I landed with only
A faint, squelching sound.

I startled a creature
That opened its beak
And ripped the night air
With a bone-jangling shriek.

Then the swamp seemed to cluster
With glittering eyes,
With lisping and slobbering
Whispers and sighs.

And a Thing shuffled forward
All hairy as doom —
The monster that came
Through the wall in my room!

"Why do you come here,
With toothbrush in hand,
To visit our swampish,
Mysterial land?"

I trembled with fear —
I could almost have died —
But I coughed in my hand
And I bravely replied,

"You came through my wall,
You came through my wall,
Horrible, horrible,
Hairy and all.

You came through my wall,
But you did not explain
How I was ever to
Find you again."

"It's easy," he breathed.
"You just give a wild call,
Take one step backward,
And jump through your wall."

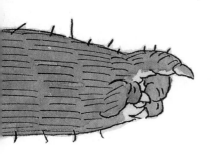

"Yes, I know that," I answered.
"That's just how I came,
But I wanted to know
Your address and your name.

I might want, for example,
To ask you to see
A movie or something that's
Good on TV."

It was all very somber,
And all very hairy,
All very swampish,
And all very scary.

"I have no address,"
The Thing finally sighed.
"And as for a name,
I am nameless," he cried.

And a look of great sorrow
Darkened his face,
As a hush fell upon
The mysterial place.

"This is his sadness,"
Explained something small.
"For lacking a name,
He is no one at all."

"Then call yourself Nameless,"
I suddenly said.
"Or something more posh, like
The Great Nameless Dread!"

The monster reared up
To a hideous height.
He gave a loud cheer
And a whoop of delight.

And all of the creatures
In sight formed a ring
'Round the monster himself
Who now started to sing.

"It is just as I thought.
It is just as he said.
I'm not no one at all,
I'm the Great Nameless Dread!"

They sang themselves silly.
They danced 'til they dropped,
While the Nameless Dread faltered
And suddenly stopped.

"You gave me a name,
Now let us adjourn.
I propose that I give you
A gift in return."

He led me away,
Through the darkening night,
To find a mysterial
Glimmer of light

Which he offered to me
With a huge, hairy fist,
While the swamp was engulfed
By mysterial mist.

Shadows and vapors
Enfolded the track
That snaked through the swamp
As we made our way back.

"Now I bid you farewell,"
I heard the Thing call,
And with light in my hand,
I walked back through my wall.

Back through the wall!
Back through the wall!
With toothbrush, pajamas,
And slippers, and all!

Back through the wall,
Feeling dizzy and dazed,
Very exhausted,
And very amazed.

Back to my bed
Where I lay in a heap,
Yawned at the ceiling,
And fell fast asleep.

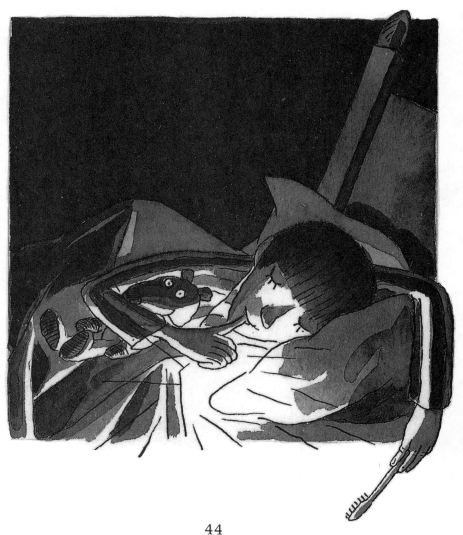

PART 3

It's sad to relate,
But, try as I might,
I never saw Nameless
After that night.

It was pretty annoying —
It really did rankle —
I leaped at the wall,
But just twisted my ankle!

Whatever I planned
Or attempted to do,
I never got back
And he never came through.

The adventure was over
And though it might seem
That the whole thing had been
Nothing more than a dream,

There's something I keep
In a drawer in my room
That I look at whenever
I'm plunged into gloom.

Whatever the problem,
By day or by night,
I look at the swampish
Mysterial light.

I look at the light
And I fondly recall
The Great Nameless Dread
That once walked through my wall.